A Dollop of Ghee
and a Pot of Wisdom

A Dollop of Ghee and a Pot of Wisdom

Stories from India

CHITRA SOUNDAR

illustrated by UMA KRISHNASWAMY

WALKER
BOOKS

To my grandmother, my first storyteller
C.S.

To Jacky Paynter, the designer,
for quiet support, thoughtful insights
U.K.

First published 2010 by Walker Books Ltd
87 Vauxhall Walk, London SE11 5HJ

2 4 6 8 10 9 7 5 3 1

Text © 2010 Chitra Soundararajan
Illustrations © 2010 Uma Krishnaswamy

The right of Chitra Soundararajan and Uma Krishnaswamy to be
identified as author and illustrator respectively of this work
has been asserted by them in accordance with the Copyright,
Designs and Patents Act 1988

This book has been typeset in StempelSchneidler

Printed in Great Britain by Clays Ltd, St Ives plc

British Library Cataloguing in Publication Data:
a catalogue record for this book is available from the British Library

ISBN 978-1-4063-1702-2

www.walker.co.uk

Contents

Prince Veera's First Case

Long ago in a faraway land, King Bheema ruled a small kingdom surrounded by the magnificent hills of Himtuk. King Bheema was a kind and just ruler. Every day he held court at the palace. Rich or poor, tall or short, man or woman – anyone could walk in with a problem. The king would always find a way to solve it.

The king lived with his beautiful wife and son in a red-stone palace. Prince Veera was ten years old. But he didn't go to school – the school came to him. His teachers lived in the palace and taught him mathematics, science, economics and many languages, including Persian, Mandarin and Latin. The prince had to master archery, horse-riding and swimming. Sons of ministers and students with special scholarships came to the palace to study with him.

If anyone could compete with Prince Veera, it was Suku, the farmer's son. Suku had won a scholarship to study with the prince. He was a good match for Veera and could tackle him in wrestling or fencing. He rode horses as well as Veera too.

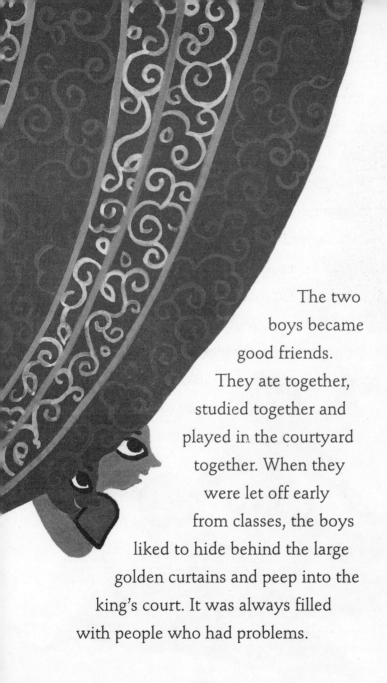

The two
boys became
good friends.
They ate together,
studied together and
played in the courtyard
together. When they
were let off early
from classes, the boys
liked to hide behind the large
golden curtains and peep into the
king's court. It was always filled
with people who had problems.

Three days after
harvest, Suku came
to the palace to
see Prince Veera. He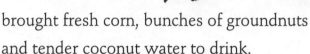
brought fresh corn, bunches of groundnuts
and tender coconut water to drink.

"Do you want to go to the woods?" Prince
Veera asked. "We can check mongoose holes
for snakes and chase deer and bison."

"After a week of harvest, I don't want to
be anywhere near plants and trees," said

Suku. "Can we sneak
into the court and see
what's going on?"

10

"Father hasn't arrived yet," said Veera. "Let's hide before he comes." He ran ahead towards the south wing.

"Where are you going?" Suku called out. "The court is this way."

"Let's go to the queen's chambers," said Veera. "We can watch the court through the small windows."

The boys scampered through the rooms, jumping onto ornate chests. The thick carpets hid the sound of their hurrying feet. Whenever a guard appeared, they hid behind the large carved doors. As soon as they reached the queen's chambers, Veera peeked in to see if any of his mother's

maids were there with the flowers and perfume the queen needed for her bath.

11

Seeing no one, the boys went through the recreation room and into the viewing gallery. The long, thin corridor overlooked the court. Alongside the windows, a bench was set up for the queen to sit on and listen. The round windows were decorated with carvings of peacocks and elephants. They glistened, reflecting the sparkle of the gemstones.

"This is a great place to spy," said Prince Veera. "You can watch and hear everything that happens."

"Shh!" Suku whispered. "Spies don't chatter."

Before Veera could reply, a horn blared.
He and Suku kneeled on the cushioned
benches and peeped through the windows.
To the beat of drums, King Bheema entered
through the large doors. Two soldiers
walked in front of him. A long train of
maroon silk stretched from the king's tunic.

"What if the sentry steps on it?" Prince
Veera asked.

"I'll die laughing," said Suku.

"I'm sure you *will* die if you laugh," said
Prince Veera. "Want to try?"

"Shh! Stop talking," said Suku.

From below they heard the king say, "Let the proceedings begin." Then King Bheema sat down on his throne.

A man stepped to the centre of the court and gave his name. He asked the king to do something about the crows that dirtied his newly built terrace.

As people presented their problems, the king sometimes asked them to come back later with more details or to bring a witness. Sometimes he gave them work, sometimes he gave them money. One or two even got punished for wasting his time.

Some of the problems were serious. One man was there about his sick parents. A woman came to complain about her greedy landlord.

Some people had silly problems – like the man who had lost his shadow. Another

wanted to charge
rent to the
birds that sat on his
roof. A woman came to
complain that the roadside
tree gave
more shade to
her neighbour's
house than her own.

"That's ridiculous," said Suku
when a man asked if he could live
inside his neighbour's chimney.

"I'm sure *we* could solve these
problems," said Veera.

"And who's going to let us?"
Suku said.

That evening the boys didn't play in the
woods or swim in the river. They played
court instead. Prince Veera met imaginary
people and heard their cases. Suku was his
counsel.

A week had
gone by. There were no classes
on New Moon day. With nothing to do, the
boys crept into the palace to watch King
Bheema hold court.

But this time, the court was empty, and
outside there was a long queue of people
waiting to see the king.

"Where is your father?" Suku asked.

Veera and Suku raced to the king's
chambers.

"The king is unwell," said the royal
physician. "Don't bother him."

Veera looked at his father's pale face. His
mother, the queen, sat close by, tending to
him.

"But people are waiting," Veera whispered to Suku.

"Maybe we should open our own court," Suku whispered back.

Veera's eyes twinkled. "This is the perfect opportunity."

He leaned towards his father's bed. "Father, I can hold court today on your behalf," he said.

"What?" the king sputtered, trying to sit up.

"We have been listening to your court for many days," admitted Veera. "We're sure we can handle it."

"Are you trying to become king?" asked the king, smiling.

"No, Father, but I will learn to govern," said Veera, "and you can get some rest."

"Well, that sounds very tempting," the king said. "But you can't do this on your own."

"Here I present to you my wise counsel, Suku," said Veera.

The king smiled at both of them. "You've been planning this for a long time then," he said. "Very well. I'll give you a chance. But you can hear only simple cases and only in the courtyard. Not in my court."

"Anything you say, Father," Veera said, unable to hide his smile.

A court was
set up quickly in the courtyard.
Prince Veera's chair was placed in the
middle. A chair for Suku was placed to its
right. Four sentries stood near by, guarding
the courtyard as people formed a queue.
Some people were alone, some had brought
their friends. Some were empty-handed.
Some held chickens or eggs, and one even
held a bucket of biriyani.

A sentry announced the arrival of the
prince. A loud gasp rose from the people.
"Where is the king?" many of them cried.

"Let's hear the first case," said the prince, sitting down.

A man who smelled of hay stepped forward and bowed to the prince. "Your Highness," he began, "my neighbour follows my cow all round town and picks up the cow dung. I want you to forbid him to do that. Anything that the cow drops belongs to me."

Veera thought about it for a moment and said, "From today, why don't you tie a dung bag behind the cow? Then you can collect all the droppings yourself."

"Next case!" said Suku.

"Dear Prince," said the next man who stepped forward. "It's my neighbour. I want her to stop singing."

"Is she awful?" asked Veera.

"She is the best singer in this city, Your Highness," he explained. "I just sit next to the window all day and listen. I miss work on most days."

Veera and Suku huddled and discussed the case.

"From today onwards, you have to keep your windows shut until you come back from work," Veera ordered.

"Who is next?" asked Suku.

Two men stepped forward, one was
dressed in cotton and the other in silk. The
first man stood with his arms folded. The
second man leaned on his wooden cane and
stroked his moustache.

"State your case," said Prince Veera.

"With due respect, dear Prince, I think
this problem is too tricky for you," said the
second man.

"If I decide the problem is too big for me, the king will surely talk to you tomorrow," said the prince. "Today you must place your trust in me."

"My name is Meetaram. I have a small sweet shop in the market. I make all the sweets myself and I use only pure butter and sugar."

"This is the prince's court. Don't waste our time talking about your sweet shop," said Suku.

"I really like sweets," said the prince. "I want to hear more."

"Your Majesty, we make laddus, jalebis, and kheer and soan papdi. We make all sorts of sweets. We are famous all over the kingdom."

"Have you brought any sweets with you?" asked the prince.

Meetaram turned and gestured to someone. Another man entered and handed

Meetaram a large plate covered by a checked cloth. The smell of sugar and butter wafted all over the courtyard. The people closed their eyes and enjoyed the smell.

"Very nice!" said the prince. "It smells very nice." He leaned forward to take a sweet.

Suku shook his head ever so slightly. Veera sat back in his chair, frowning at Suku.

"Don't smell it, Your Majesty," said the other man. "That's exactly the problem."

"Take the sweets to my room," Veera said.

A sentry took the plate from Meetaram.

"Your Majesty, this man, Kapi, stood

several minutes outside my shop smelling my sweets. But he left without buying or paying."

"If he didn't buy, why must he pay?" asked Veera.

"Because he enjoyed the smell so much. It takes a lot of butter and sugar to get that smell, Your Majesty. That smell attracts many customers into the shop. If they all came just to smell my sweets and never buy any, I wouldn't make any money."

"Hmmm, interesting," said the prince.

"This man Kapi should pay five silver coins for enjoying the sweet smells in my shop. You have to be fair, Prince Veera, just like your father."

Prince Veera closed his eyes. He could almost touch the wafting fragrance of the sweets. It made him slightly hungry.

"Kapi, what do you say for yourself?"

Kapi was not as richly dressed as Meetaram. He was thin and didn't wear any jewellery. His white shirt was almost brown and his dhoti was patched in many places.

"My dear prince, I'm a poor man," Kapi began. "I work very hard in the fields. Once a month, I come to town to buy groceries. I have only five silver coins. Walking through the market, I smelled the sweets. I stopped for a few minutes, taking in the wonderful smells. But the sweets were too expensive. I couldn't afford to buy rice, vegetables *and* sweets with the money I had."

"What did you do then?" asked the prince. He didn't realize that people had to choose between vegetables and sweets. He was surprised that Kapi decided to buy vegetables instead of sweets. I'd definitely choose the sweets, he thought.

"My children need food, Your Majesty. They go to school and they need to eat well. The sweets would last for just a day. But the rice and vegetables will last all month. So I decided not to buy the sweets."

"But you enjoyed the smell?" the prince asked.

"Yes, I did. Somehow the smell itself was enough. It felt like eating the sweets."

"That's exactly my case, Your Majesty," piped in Meetaram.

"Shh!" Suku hushed the man.

The prince closed his eyes. He tried not to think about the sweets, just the problem in front of him. What would Father do?

"OK, I've decided," said Prince Veera. "Kapi, give your five silver coins to Meetaram."

Kapi's face fell. With tears in his eyes, he handed over the money.

Meetaram's face lit up with joy. He counted the five silver coins at least five times.

The prince watched this in silence.

"Thank you, dear prince. You are very fair and just," said Meetaram. "I'll take my leave now."

"Not so fast, my man. Now please return the five silvers to Kapi."

"But—"

"Well, he smelled your sweets, but he didn't eat them."

"Yes, but—"

"And you held the money in your hands, didn't you?"

"Yes, but—"

"You counted it; you imagined adding it to your moneybox. You enjoyed that, didn't you?"

"Yes, but—"

"He enjoyed the smell of sweets and you enjoyed the feel of money. A fair exchange, don't you think?"

Meetaram hung his head in shame.

"From now on, treat your customers fairly," Prince Veera cautioned. "Always make some sweets for people who cannot afford to buy expensive ones."

Meetaram returned the money and left the court.

"Bring the plate of sweets from my room," said the prince. "Take these to your children, Kapi. Let them eat rice, vegetables *and* sweets today."

Kapi left the court smiling and carrying a large basket filled with sweets.

That night during dinner, Prince Veera ate all his vegetables, even his peas.

Who Stole the Laddus?

Ever since Meetaram brought the sweets into the court, not a meal was eaten without discussing them. The cooks, sentries, maids – everyone talked about the sweets and the fragrance that lingered in the hallways.

"Maybe the prince should have given the sweets to everyone," said a sentry.

"Maybe the prince should have fined Meetaram and made him bring more sweets," said another.

Prince Veera, too, found it difficult to forget the aroma of the sweets. He ordered that the palace be sprayed with camphor fumes to wipe out the wafting smell. But it didn't help. The smell was lodged in everyone's minds. Wiping it out of the courtyard, thrones, curtains and carpets didn't make it go away.

The news reached the ministers, then the queen and king.

"What is this gossip about sweets?" King Bheema asked.

"It's nothing, Father. Just a case," said Prince Veera.

"Was the smell really divine?" asked the queen.

"Yes, it was. Not even the royal cook has made sweets that smelled like that."

"Your father loves sweets," said the queen. "Especially those made of butter! The laddus, that's his favourite."

"Maybe we should order some sweets," said the king. "If only I'd handled this case before I let you have your own court!"

"Let me check that Meetaram is not cheating anyone now. If he has reformed his ways, then you can buy sweets from his shop," Prince Veera said. He didn't want Meetaram to use his court to sell more sweets.

So the next day, the prince set out to the market dressed like an urchin.

"Can you find the shop on your own?" asked the queen.

"I'll ask around," said Prince Veera. But he didn't have to. The buttery, sugary smell wafted through the market, telling him where to go.

Veera sat outside the sweet shop for hours, smelling the cinnamon, cardamom and cashews. He watched the customers come in and saw that Meetaram was fair to them. He looked at the plates on the shelves, loaded with sweets. He licked his lips but he bought nothing.

After sunset Meetaram closed his shop
and Prince Veera returned to the palace,
hungry, tired and hot. It is hard business,
this justice, he thought. But it was good to
know that Meetaram had indeed mended
his ways.

Next day, the prince sent a sentry with a
large cart down to the market. The king had
written down his order for the sweets and
so had the queen. Prince Veera and Suku
wanted some too. Every member of the
royal household wanted the sweets.

Meetaram was delighted. He checked the list many times. He loaded the cart with sweets. "These are for the king, the queen and the prince," he said. "I will personally deliver the rest by tomorrow. First we have to make a new batch."

"That means the rest of us will have to wait another day," said the sentry, and he drove the cart back towards the palace.

Back at the palace, the royal family were waiting. As soon as the cart arrived, the sweets were unloaded and brought to the kitchen.

The king stepped forward and opened a large box of laddus. The yellow balls of

lentils fried in sugar syrup
glistened in the light.

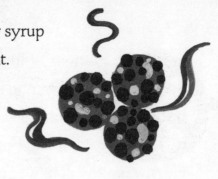

"*Svadishta!*
Delicious!" he
cried, biting into
a big laddu.

Just as he finished the first and reached for
a second, the minister arrived. "A messenger
from the kingdom of Chalu is here to see
you, Your Majesty," he said.

"Not now!" the king bellowed.

"Sorry, Your Majesty. This is of utmost
importance."

The king put the box down on
the table. There were
exactly eleven laddus
left. "Don't smell
them and don't
touch them,"
he warned.
"And don't eat them!"

* * *

Early next morning, Prince Veera was
awakened by a loud noise. He stumbled
out of bed and went to the door. What was
it? It was not thunder, but more like a roar.
He opened the door and listened intently.
It sounded like his father. But King Bheema
never shouted – at least, not that early in the
morning! The sun had not even risen high
enough to warm the pond in the garden.

Prince Veera slipped out of his room and
followed the sound. Father was not in his
room. He was not in the courtyard.
Father was not in the
grounds or anywhere
near the pond.

Where could
he be?

Prince Veera
listened hard.
The sound

came from the far east wing of the palace, by the royal kitchen. What was Father doing in the kitchen? He hardly ever went there, unless he didn't want anyone to know he was eating.

Then Veera remembered the sweets, the sweets that Father had to abandon until his official duties were over! Veera walked swiftly to the kitchen.

A crowd of servants stood outside, their ears to the door. Inside the king ranted and raved. When Prince Veera walked closer, the servants moved away.

"What's going on?" Veera asked.

"It's about the laddu," said one of the maids.

"One laddu? Is that the reason for his anger?"

I handled the case and I brought the fragrance into the palace, Veera thought. Oh, my sweet butters, what's going to happen to me?

"One laddu is missing," said the maid. "The king left exactly eleven of them in the box last night. This morning, when he came by, only ten remained."

"Do you know who took the missing laddu?"

"No one knows. Nobody will own up."

Prince Veera smiled. This was something he could handle. Well, the laddu had gone missing. It would

never come back, but the memory of its
fragrance and its taste would never leave the
mind of the person who had eaten it. "Time
for me to sort this out," he said as he pushed
the door open and went into the kitchen.

Inside he saw that the king
was still in his pyjamas,
standing on top of a huge
cauldron. His face was
red. The kitchen
staff stood in front
of him, shaking like
flags on a windy day.

"Father, what is the problem?" Veera asked.

The king stopped his tirade and looked at his son. "I want to know who is lying. I can forgive stealing, but not lying."

"Why not leave this to me?" said the prince. "I'll find out."

"This is all because of your case," said the king. "We were happy before we knew about Meetaram's sweets."

Prince Veera hung his head. The sooner he found the culprit, the better it would be  for everyone. He plucked up his courage and looked up. "Father, you have many appointments today. Why don't you get ready

while I solve this problem? I'll bring the culprit to your court."

King Bheema picked up the box of laddus. "I'm not leaving this here any longer. Lock it up in a cupboard," he told his personal guard, then he left.

Prince Veera smiled. "Remember," he said to everyone. "You are in this kitchen to cook food, not steal it. The sooner we get to the bottom of this, the sooner we can all get back to cooking breakfast and lunch. I say this because I'm very hungry and I can't wait very long."

No one stirred. The thief was lying low.

"I know the sweets are very tempting and the smell makes you hungry, but it is not good to lie to the king," said Prince Veera. "Now, who took the laddu?"

No one would own up. Not a single word was spoken. Prince Veera didn't know who the thief could be.

"I'll tell the king to forgive you," said the prince, "but you must confess now."

Again no one stepped forward.

"Then it is time to invoke the God of Honesty," the prince said, signalling to the sentry. "Please fetch me twenty pieces of firewood of the same length."

In a few minutes, the sentry returned with an armload of firewood.

"Each of you gets one piece of wood," said the prince. "You will step through the pantry invoking the God of Honesty and pray for mercy. Then you will come out the other side."

Everyone nodded.

"Remember, if you are speaking the truth, your firewood will shrink by an inch by the time you step out the other side. If you are

lying, the God of Honesty will not grace you with his presence and your stick will remain the same length."

The sentry handed out the sticks as each person walked through the pantry. The prince stood waiting on the other side.

As they walked in, each of them chanted the familiar slogan – *"Satyameva Jayete!"* – invoking the God of Honesty. Then they stepped out of the pantry and stood in front of the prince with their piece of wood.

"Measure each of these," Veera ordered.

The sentry measured each piece of firewood and noted the measurements on a scroll.

Prince Veera then read through the scroll and smiled. "I know who did it. Tell the king we will be in his court shortly."

But the king didn't wait for Veera. He wanted to know who had lied to him. He came to the kitchen straight away.

"Do you know who did it?" asked the king.

"Yes, Father. I know who stole the laddu and who lied to us," said the prince.

"I'll forgive the stealing. The laddu is not important. We're getting another cartload today. But who lied to me?"

"The fourth man from the left," said Prince Veera.

Before the king could say anything, the liar fell at the king's feet. "I am sorry, Your Majesty. I won't lie to you ever again."

"Take him away, we'll deal with him

later," said the king. "How did you find this out, Veera?"

"I merely invoked the conscience in the guilty man," Prince Veera said.

"Did you threaten him?" asked the king.

"Father, I did no such thing," said Veera, and he explained what he had made the servants do.

"How will that help? Did the guilty man confess?"

"No, Father. The servants believed that the God of Honesty would shrink their firewood if they were innocent. Because the God of Honesty would not help him, the guilty man was afraid that his firewood would be longer than the others."

The king nodded with his eyes closed. He understood the minds of the wrongdoers. They always lived in fear of being found out.

"The culprit took a knife and chopped a small bit of the firewood. So when we measured all of the pieces at the end, the one with the shortest firewood was the liar." Prince Veera held up the scroll.

"Well done, my son. The laddu thief was caught by his own guilty conscience."

"So can I share a laddu with you, Father?" Veera asked.

"Of course you can, my son," the king said. "Can I share one of your jalebis?"

The Case of the
Greedy Moneylender

Prince Veera had a busy schedule during the day. He had to get up very early to go swimming. After breakfast he studied mathematics, science and economics. After lunch he practised archery, horse-riding and wrestling.

One Wednesday, Suku was expected to join Veera for his morning swim. Veera waited at the riverbank, but there was no sign of his friend. Veera swam alone.

He expected Suku to join him for breakfast, but again he was disappointed.

"Where is Suku?" Veera asked his mother.

"Maybe he is needed at the farm today, son," said the queen.

The whole day passed and there was no sign of Suku. Veera couldn't wait any longer. He decided to go and find him.

Veera rode his white horse through the wide streets of Himpur. His personal guards rode behind him. The streets were lined with neem and banyan trees. Veera went past the village temple,

the lotus lake
and then
crossed the
bridge over
the lake. The streets
were narrower now
and the houses smaller.
Large corn and paddy
fields were dotted with farmhouses.

"Look, the prince is here
to see Suku," said a man
looking up from his work.

The people who lived in
Suku's neighbourhood were
not surprised. Veera came often to visit Suku
and spent a lot of time playing in the streets.
If he was not wearing expensive clothes or
jewellery, or if there were no guards around
the area, they would not realize it was
Prince Veera playing hide and seek on the
streets with the other boys.

Veera dismounted from his horse outside Suku's parents' house. He knocked on the door and Suku's father opened it.

"Welcome, my dear prince," said Suku's father.

"Good evening, sir. Where is my friend, Suku?" asked the prince.

"He has gone away on a short trip," said Suku's father.

"What sort of trip?" asked the prince. "He never mentioned anything."

"It was quite sudden, Your Majesty. He had to leave this morning."

56

Prince Veera looked around. Suku's clothes were still there. His bag and shoes were there too. "All his things are here," he said. "Please tell me what is going on."

Suku's father couldn't hold back his tears any longer. "The greedy moneylender has taken my boy away, Your Majesty. I didn't want to burden you with my problems. Neither did Suku."

"How much do you owe the moneylender?" Prince Veera.

"Twenty-five silvers. Just twenty-five silvers. But I don't have that money. Not until I complete my harvest and sell my crops in the market."

"Who is this moneylender?" asked the prince. "He is very heartless."

"Angar is his name," said Suku's father, and he explained.

"Angar comes from a family of moneylenders. He charges heavy interest on the money he lends. He even leases utensils and jewellery for weddings. And he takes away people's belongings when they are

unable to pay the interest. He is very greedy, Your Majesty."

"I'm going to do something about this," said the prince.

"But Suku is still with him," said Suku's father. "I don't want to cause any trouble. I don't want anything to happen to my son, Your Majesty."

"Get me a bag of twenty-five silvers," Veera said to his guard, "and get my friend back." Then, to Suku's parents he said, "I'll teach the moneylender a lesson he will never forget."

Suku's parents refused the money at first, but Prince Veera urged them to take it. After a lot of discussion, they finally agreed to accept the prince's help in bringing their son back.

Next day Suku returned home from the moneylender's, then headed straight to the palace with a bag of sweet potatoes and guavas.

"Thank you," he said. "You have been very kind to us. My father will repay the money after the harvest."

"Never mind, Suku," said Prince Veera. "I couldn't wait until the harvest to beat you at horse-riding or archery, could I?"

"Ha! To be beaten, you mean!" said Suku. "You can't wait to lose."

"We'll see about that. What happened at the moneylender's house?" asked the prince. "Did he hurt you at all?"

"No, he just made me do all his chores," said Suku. "He made me count the money, make tea for him and even wash his clothes. But that was easy. He had only two pairs of shirts and two dhotis."

"Didn't you say he was rich?"

"Yes, he is. But he doesn't spend money. He eats only one meal a day, to save his silvers."

"That is pure greed," said Prince Veera. "Maybe he is saving the money for a reason."

"I don't think any reason is good enough to swindle people out of their possessions," said Suku. "He makes people give up their hard-earned things and money just to fill his coffers."

"Does he have any children?"

"No children, no family," said Suku. "Not even a pet. He lives alone, counts his money, eats, sleeps and snores. He doesn't even have a bailiff to collect his dues. If people return the money late, he charges more interest."

"We have to teach him a lesson, my friend," said Prince Veera. "We can't let him continue to cheat any more."

"You mean, report him to your father's court?" asked Suku. "I don't think we can do that. People who borrow from him sign on a paper that says they agree to his terms. Your father will throw the case out when he sees the papers."

"But that's not fair," said the prince. "We have to teach him a lesson. How about a bit of Veera treatment? Are you ready for some fun?"

Then Veera whispered a plan to his friend.

Next day, dressed as an ordinary farmer's boy, Veera set off to see the moneylender. No one noticed him as he walked down the street

and turned right
at the village square,
into a road lined with
beautiful magnolia trees.

The fragrance was wonderful.

Angar the moneylender lived at number
77. A large statue of a white elephant stood
outside the door.

No one could
miss that,
thought Veera
as he knocked.

A thin,
scrawny man
opened the door.

"I'm here to see Angar, the moneylender,"
said Veera.

"What for?" barked the man.

"To borrow some utensils for my sister's
wedding."

"Come in," said the man.

Veera stepped inside. The house was
large and spacious, but he noticed that there
wasn't any furniture, except for a desk set
up on a dais. The seating area was covered
in silk. There wasn't a single chair to sit on.

The man climbed onto the dais and sat
down on the silk-covered floor.

"I am Angar," he said. "What kind of
pots and pans do you need?"

"Can I look at them and decide?"
asked Veera.

64

The moneylender pointed to a green door. Veera pushed it open and stepped inside a room filled with pots, pans, ladles and cups. They were made of copper, bronze and steel, and some were made of earthenware.

Veera took a selection of bronze vessels and stepped out again. He put them on the floor and said, "These are the ones I need."

"Very well then. You are taking ten pots. You must return them in the same condition in a week's time. You owe me three silvers now and two silvers when you return them." The moneylender wrote down the details in his notebook.

Veera handed three silvers to the moneylender, took his pots and left.

One week went by and then two. A whole month had passed and still Veera hadn't bothered to return the pots.

"I think we have waited long enough," said Suku. "We should return the pots to the moneylender."

"Angar must have forgotten about them by now," said Veera. "He hasn't sent anyone to get them."

"He doesn't do that," explained Suku. "He simply charges more. Make sure you bring some extra silvers with you."

"Don't worry, my friend," said Veera. "I have enough to keep Angar happy."

He carefully lifted twenty pots and placed them in a bullock cart.

Suku drove the cart while Veera sat inside, holding the pots. The boys arrived at the moneylender's house and unloaded the cart.

On hearing them, Angar appeared from inside.

"Where were you all this time?" he yelled. "You should have returned these pots weeks ago. I will have to charge you more now."

Veera smiled. "Well, kind sir, there is a small problem. You asked me to return the pots in the same condition. But I'm afraid that is not possible."

"Why not? Did you break them? How did you break bronze pots?"

"I didn't break them," said Veera. "But, you see, these pots gave birth to little ones. They were in a delicate state. I couldn't bring them until the little pots were strong enough to travel."

"Strong enough?" asked the moneylender. "What are you talking about?"

"See, dear sir, you didn't realize that the pots you lent to me were with children," explained Veera. "After the wedding was over, I had left them in the pantry for just a few hours. Then I heard sounds. Sounds of the pots rattling and clanging. When I rushed in to check, there were little pots in them."

"I don't believe this," said Angar.

"I knew you'd say that," said the prince. "Here, I brought your pots with their little ones. They all belong to you rightfully."

Angar counted the big pots. There were ten. He counted the small pots. There were ten. Well, what a neat profit!

"Thank you, young man," he said. "You're very honest. Others would have hidden the little pots and never returned them."

Even though Angar was happy with the little pots, he still charged Veera for the delay in returning the large ones. Veera forked out five silvers and returned home with Suku.

"I couldn't believe it when he actually stroked the little pots with love," said Suku. "That man is so greedy."

"Let him enjoy his pots while he can," said Veera. His eyes glinted at the prospect of teaching Angar a lesson. No one mistreated his friend and got away with it!

A week later, again dressed in ordinary clothes, Veera set off to see the moneylender. This time he needed no introduction. When he asked for twenty pots, the moneylender was more than happy to lend them.

"Please take as many as you like. Remember to bring back any little ones," he said, giving him a receipt for six silvers.

Veera returned home and sent the pots to the royal kitchen. They weren't going anywhere again. Suku and Veera continued with their lessons for a month before they remembered Angar and his pots.

"Now that we are done with our lessons, do you think Angar is ready for his?" Suku asked.

"That sounds like fun," said Veera, and they discussed what they would tell Angar.

Veera and Suku set off on their horses, but they dismounted before they reached Angar's house. They walked up to the door and knocked.

When the door opened, Veera and Suku burst out crying. They sat on the doorstep and cried loudly. They wailed and screamed. The whole street came to watch.

"What's wrong with you?" asked Angar. "Why are you crying?"

"It's about the pots. I can't bear to tell you," said the prince.

"What about the pots?"

"You see, they are bronze pots. They were very old."

"I know! They are my family heirlooms. Irreplaceable. If I had to buy them now, it would cost me at least five hundred silvers."

On hearing this, Veera and Suku sobbed more.

"Tell me what's wrong," Angar said.

"Do you remember these pots gave birth to the little ones last month?" asked Veera.

"I remember. What happened now?"

"Well, the pots must have been very ill. Didn't you take care of them properly? After we put them in the pantry, there was no noise. I went to check on them. But unfortunately they were all dead."

"Dead?"

"Yes, the pots died yesterday at dawn!" cried Veera. "I'm so sorry."

"How can the pots die? They are made of bronze." Angar threw up his hands in despair.

"Well, if they can give birth to little bronze pots, can't they die too?" asked Suku.

Angar had no answer to this. He hung his head in shame. The whole street laughed at his misery.

From that day onwards, Angar stopped being greedy. He charged fair interest and he never unjustly took away things – or children – from anyone again.

The Unfortunate Case

It was a hot summer. No one in the kingdom studied during the hottest months. The sun scorched the earth. Lakes and streams dried up. The children were allowed to play outdoors only until noon and then again at dusk. They had to remain indoors during the afternoon.

Prince Veera and Suku spent their time in the mangroves near the palace. The grove was shady and cool. The boys climbed trees,

chased dragonflies and
feasted on juicy mangoes.
A river ran right through
the grove that was fed
from the beautiful hills
of Himtuk and it
never dried up.
After a long
day of playing,
the boys were
tired. The sun
was setting
and it was the
right time to get
something to eat.

"Let's go to the palace and
raid the kitchen," said Veera.

"That's what we always
do," said Suku. "Why don't
we go to the marketplace
today?"

Prince Veera never turned down an opportunity to mingle with his people. He preferred to roam the streets than travel in style in a carriage. "Let's do that," he said.

So the boys set off to the market with a silver coin each. A guard dressed in plain clothes followed them at a discreet distance.

The market was bustling with people. The stalls were filled with fruits, vegetables, sweets and cold drinks.

One man sold tender coconut water and another sold palm fruits. A woman sold buttermilk from a huge mud pot.

People came to the market on horses and donkeys and in bullock carts.

The sound of
animals mingled
with the noise of
the vendors and
the bells from the
temple nearby.

Prince Veera enjoyed
his visits to the market.
It was much more
exciting than the
palace.

Suku and Veera
wandered around,
trying on hats,
eating mangoes
and drinking
coconut milk.

As they
approached the
village square, people
were whispering.

Suku spotted a man under a banyan tree. The man was dressed in rags and he carried a dirty cotton bag.

"What is it?" the prince asked. "Why are people whispering?"

"Nothing, my friend. Let's go to the other street," Suku said, steering Veera away. Then, "Pschckkk!"

Prince Veera turned and saw the look of dismay on his friend's face. He burst out laughing. Suku had stepped in horse manure. He held up his leg and hopped around. "You never watch where you walk," Veera said.

"It's not my fault!" cried Suku. "It is all because of the bad luck that man spreads."

"Why are you blaming a stranger, Suku?" asked Veera.

Suku didn't reply. He approached a nearby shop and asked the shopkeeper for a pot of water to clean his shoes. "Let's go," he said.

Even after they returned to the palace, Prince Veera couldn't help thinking about the incident in the market. "Are you going to tell me or not?" he asked. "Why did you blame the man from the market?"

"I don't want to share bad luck, Veera," said Suku. "Why don't you just let it go?"

"I thought you knew me better," said Veera.

"I will tell you then," said Suku. "The man's name is Dhuri. He spreads bad luck throughout the kingdom."

"How could someone spread bad luck?" asked Veera. "What does he do?"

"He does nothing. Just by seeing or talking to him, something bad will happen to you,"

Suku explained, still examining his shoes for specks of horse manure.

"I'm sure that is just superstition," said Veera.

"Not at all. I stepped on horse manure as soon as I saw him."

"That was because you never watch where you walk," said Veera. "You were slurping on the juicy mangoes."

"I don't agree," said Suku. "It's all bad luck. And that man is spreading it."

Prince Veera argued hard and long with Suku, but they got nowhere. "Let's ask my father," he suggested.

"Don't do that, Veera. The king will want to meet this man. What if something bad happens to the king?"

"A king should meet all his subjects," said the prince. "He cannot discriminate."

So they took their problem to the king. King Bheema listened carefully. Then he had a word with his ministers. Everyone agreed that Suku was right. This man Dhuri did spread bad luck.

"Interesting," said the king. "I wish to see him tomorrow."

Next morning, while the king was getting dressed, he looked out of the window. The guards were bringing a poor, dirty man into the palace.

"Are you ready for the court, my dear?" asked the queen.

The king turned swiftly and knocked over a glass of water.

"Careful!" said the queen. "Don't be in such a hurry."

When the king sat down for breakfast, he was told that the royal chef was not feeling well. So the king was unable to eat his

favourite meal, aloo paratha – bread with spicy potato filling.

As the king approached the throne, he banged his leg and yelped in pain. Hurriedly he sat down, wishing that he had not peeped out of the window that morning and looked at that man. He wished he had listened to his ministers too. But he was the king. He had to meet everyone, even the man who spread bad luck.

"Bring in Dhuri," the king ordered.

Prince Veera and Suku stood behind the ministers and watched the proceedings. Suku shut his eyes tight and refused to look at the man even when Prince Veera nudged him.

"Dhuri, do you spread bad luck?" asked the king.

"I think I am filled with bad luck, Your Majesty," the man replied. "I have no work, no friends and no family. But I don't wish to bring ill to anyone else."

"But that's not true," said the king. "I glanced at you early this morning from my window. I knocked over a glass of water, my favourite breakfast was not ready and my toes hurt."

"Well, that could be carelessness, coincidence and haste, Your Majesty."

"Are you calling me careless and hasty?"

"Not at all, Your Majesty. It happens to the best of us," Dhuri said. "Some days are better than others."

Prince Veera smiled. This man was intelligent, courageous and articulate. It was unfortunate that no one gave him work.

"But I don't agree," said the king. "I agree with my ministers that you indeed spread bad luck. I condemn you to twenty-five years in prison so that no one will ever suffer again."

"That's not fair, Your Majesty," said Dhuri. "I didn't do anything wrong."

Prince Veera was shocked. He pulled Suku by his hand and stepped forward. "Father—Your Majesty," he began. "This is not fair."

"You are a child. Know your place," said the king.

"But you have always taught me to raise my voice against unfair things," said Veera. "This is one of them."

"This man spreads bad luck," the king said.

"But I can present to you another man who spreads more bad luck than Dhuri."

"Is there another one of these in my kingdom? Who is it?"

"You!" cried Prince Veera. "You have managed to spread more bad luck than Dhuri."

Everyone in the court gasped. They looked at the prince with horror. Suku stepped back and moved behind the curtains.

"Veera, mind your words!" said the king.

"Please listen to me, Father. You glanced at Dhuri this morning and you had these minor accidents. You blame him for all your bad luck. But Dhuri didn't even look at you this morning. He was just coming over to see you. Yet you have sentenced him to twenty-five years in prison."

Dhuri looked up and smiled.

"If you believed Dhuri caused you hardship, then it is just superstition," said Veera. "Dhuri never intended to harm you. But what you did to Dhuri is deliberate. You want him to rot in prison. It seems to me that you spread more bad luck and ill-will than he does, Father."

King Bheema closed his eyes. He nodded slowly. Then he stepped down from his throne and hugged his son.

"You're right, my son. I was swayed by my emotions. I committed an injustice. Thank you for speaking the truth and speaking it loudly." The king walked back to his throne and looked at the court.

"Here in this court, we almost fell into the traps of superstition. I apologize to Dhuri for my hasty judgement."

"I am thankful to the prince, Your Majesty," said Dhuri. "And I am grateful to you for heeding to the voices in your court. May your rule flourish and prosper."

"Dhuri, you are a free man," said the king. "The minister will help you find a job and a place to stay."

The court adjourned and Suku peeped through the curtain. "You were very brave, Veera."

"I just stood up for the right thing," said Prince Veera. "That's what princes do."

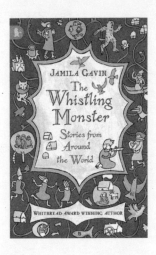

From Brazil to Botswana, Mongolia to Mexico, Finland to France, everyone loves a story! After hundreds of years of retelling, these ten tales have become favourites all around the world.

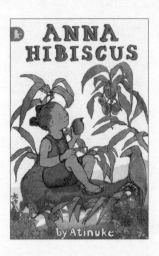

Anna Hibiscus
lives in Africa. Amazing Africa.

She lives with her whole family in
a wonderful house. There is always
somebody to laugh or play with.
She loves to splash in the sea with her
cousins and have parties for her aunties.
But more than anything else in the
world, Anna would love to see snow.

Chitra Soundar

is originally from the culturally colourful India, where traditions, festivals and mythology are a way of life. As a child, she feasted on generous portions of folktales and stories from Hindu mythology. As she grew older, she started making up her own stories. Chitra now lives in London, cramming her little flat with storybooks of all kinds.

Uma Krishnaswamy

has always loved the folk traditions of India and other cultures for the richness and vibrancy of colour, form and perspective. Coming from a culture that straddles modernity and tradition with ease, mixes regional and other flavours to spice things up, she works at reflecting these contradictory elements, hopefully with some degree of success. She also teaches art theory in Chennai, where she lives.